W9-BFR-930

An I Can Read Book®

Marvin's Best Christmas Present Ever

story by
KATHERINE PATERSON
pictures by
JANE CLARK BROWN

HarperCollins*Publishers*

This book is a presentation of Newfield Publications, Inc.
For information about Newfield Publications'
book clubs for children write to:
Newfield Publications, Inc.,
4343 Equity Drive Columbus, Ohio 43228

Published by arrangement with HarperCollins Publishers.
Newfield Publications is a federally registered
trademark of Newfield Publications, Inc.

1997 edition

For
Margaret Anne Pierce
with love from Grandpop
who discovered the secret of the wreath
and Nana who wrote about it
—K.P.

For Leah and Lindsay Brown
with love from MuMu
—J.C.B.

Marvin Gates and his family

lived in a trailer

on the Smiths' dairy farm.

One day Marvin saw Mrs. Smith hang
a wreath on the farmhouse door.
She put greens and lights
in all the windows.
Greens and lights and a wreath
meant Christmas was coming.

Marvin was worried about Christmas.

"What are you giving Mom and Dad?"

he asked his big sister, May.

“I’m making a book

of all my stories,” said May.

“I am going to draw pictures

to go with each story.

It will be a beautiful book.

They’ll keep it forever.”

Marvin sighed.

Everything May made was nice.

Mom and Dad would love her book.

Marvin could write stories,

but they were never as good as May's.

He could draw pictures,

but they were never as good as May's.

“Last year I made a macaroni necklace

for Mom,” said Marvin,

“but she never wears it anymore.

I made Dad an ashtray,

but he stopped smoking.”

May felt sorry for Marvin.

"Do you want me to help you

make a present?" she asked.

"No," said Marvin,

but he really did.

For once in his life

he wanted to make a great present.

"Christmas is coming fast,"
said Mom. "The Smiths have
a big wreath on their door."
Marvin wanted a wreath
on his house, too,
but the trailer door was too small
for a wreath.
Then Marvin had an idea.

“I can make a big wreath
and hang it on the end
of the trailer,” he said to himself.
“The wreath will be a great present.
Everyone will love it.
They will keep it forever!”

Marvin found some greens

that Mrs. Smith had left over.

He tried to tie them into a wreath,

but he couldn't do it by himself.

Finally he said to May,
"If you help me,
will it still be my present?"
"Yes," said May. "It was your idea.
So it will be your present."

Rosie

On Christmas Eve morning
Marvin and May hung the wreath
on the end of the trailer.

Dad saw it

when he came home from the barn.

“What a great wreath!” Dad said.

“Where did it come from?”

“Me!” said Marvin. “I made it.

It’s your Christmas present from me.”

Mom saw the wreath
when she came home from shopping.

“What a beautiful wreath!” she said.

“Did someone make it for us?”

“I did!” said Marvin. “May helped.”

“Yes,” said May. “I helped,

but it’s Marvin’s present.”

Everyone loved the wreath.

Marvin loved it most of all.

On New Year's Day, May said,
"Marvin, we took down the tree.
Now it's time
to take down the wreath."

"No!" said Marvin.

"It's still green.

It's still beautiful."

Mom said,

"It can stay awhile longer.

It looks so pretty on the trailer."

On Valentine's Day, May said,

"Marvin, let's make a big heart

and put it on the trailer.

I'll help you."

"No!" said Marvin.

"I want to keep my wreath there."

"It can stay awhile longer,"

said Dad. "I like looking at it."

Marvin was happy.

He liked to look at his wreath too.

He wanted to keep his wreath forever.

In March, May said,

"The wreath is getting brown.

We should take it down.

It will be Easter soon.

I'll help you make a bunny

for the trailer."

"No!" said Marvin.

"It's only a little bit brown."

"We can leave it until Easter,"

Mom said.

Easter came much too fast,

but a wonderful thing happened.

It snowed!

“Easter looks just like Christmas,”

Dad said.

“We’ll leave the wreath up

for a few more days.”

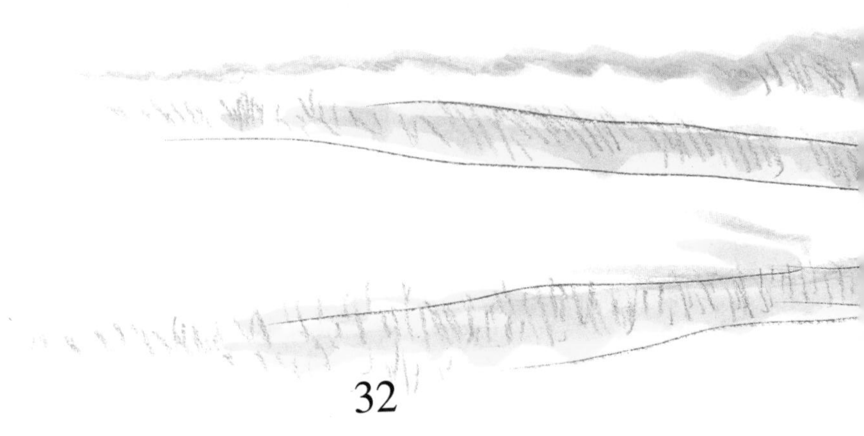

The snow melted away.

Marvin's wreath was brown and dry.

"Mom," said May.

"That wreath has got to go."

"No!" said Marvin.

Mom looked sad.
"It was a great present,"
she said.
"Dad and I loved it,
but I'm afraid May is right."
"Yes," said Dad.
"I'm afraid it's time
for the wreath to go."

Marvin felt like crying.

The wreath was the best present

he had ever made.

He didn't want it

to be thrown away.

Dad went to the trailer.

He was gone a long time.

When Dad came back he was smiling.

"Did you throw my wreath away?"

Marvin asked.

"No," said Dad.

"I couldn't throw it away."

"But Dad," May said,

"that's a Christmas wreath.

An ugly brown Christmas wreath."

Mom sighed. "I guess

we should have taken it down

long ago."

"Too late now," said Dad.

"Come and see."

SALE

Mom, May, and Marvin
followed Dad.

He tiptoed around
to the end of the trailer.

"Oh," said Mom.

"Ohh," said May.

"What is it?" asked Marvin.

Dad picked Marvin up to see.

There in the wreath

a bird had made her nest.

In the nest were six tiny eggs.

“Ohhh,” said Marvin.

“Someone else likes your wreath,”

Dad said.

"It's the best present I ever made,"

said Marvin.

"I think we should keep it forever."

"Who knows?" said Mom.

"Maybe we will."

"I wish I could make

a present like this," said May.

“I’ll help you,” said Marvin.

“I can make great presents.”